Europa and Cadmus

希臘羅馬神話故事 ❺

歐羅巴和卡德莫斯 Europa and Cadmus

First Published April, 2011
First Printing April, 2011

Original Story by Thomas Bulfinch
Rewritten by Isaac Durst
Illustrated by Gutdva Irina Mixailovna
Designer by Eonju No
Translated by Jia-chen Chuo
Printed and distributed by Cosmos Culture Ltd.
Tel: 02-2365-9739
Fax: 02-2365-9835
http://www.icosmos.com.tw
Publisher: Value-Deliver Culture Ltd.

Mythology gives you interesting explanations about life and satisfies your curiosity with stories that have been made up to explain surprising or frightening phenomena.

People throughout the world have their own myths. In the imaginary world of mythology, humans can become birds or stars. The sun, wind, trees, and the rest of the natural world are full of gods who often interact with humans.

Greek and Roman mythology began more than 3,000 years ago. It consisted of stories first told by Greeks that lived on the shores of the Mediterranean Sea. In Italy the Romans would later borrow and modify many of these stories.

Most of the Greek myths were related to gods that resided upon the cloud-shrouded Mount Olympus. These clouds frequently could create a mysterious atmosphere on Mount Olympus. The ancient Greeks thought that their gods dwelt there and had human

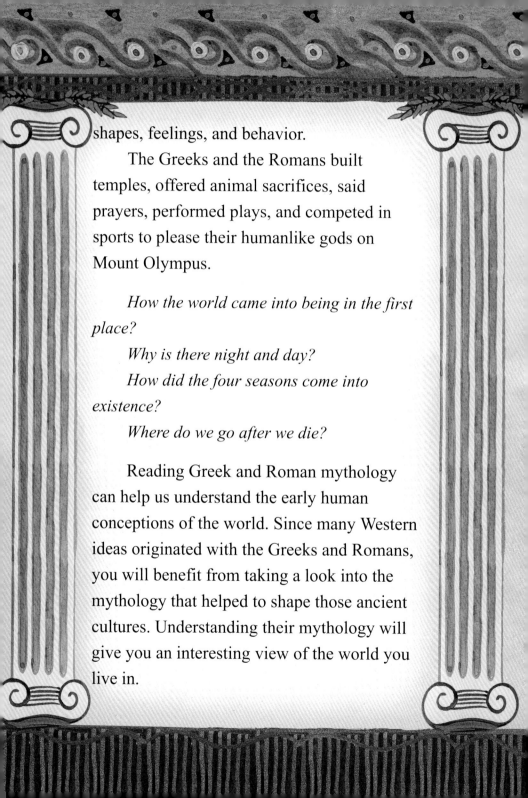

shapes, feelings, and behavior.

The Greeks and the Romans built temples, offered animal sacrifices, said prayers, performed plays, and competed in sports to please their humanlike gods on Mount Olympus.

How the world came into being in the first place?

Why is there night and day?

How did the four seasons come into existence?

Where do we go after we die?

Reading Greek and Roman mythology can help us understand the early human conceptions of the world. Since many Western ideas originated with the Greeks and Romans, you will benefit from taking a look into the mythology that helped to shape those ancient cultures. Understanding their mythology will give you an interesting view of the world you live in.

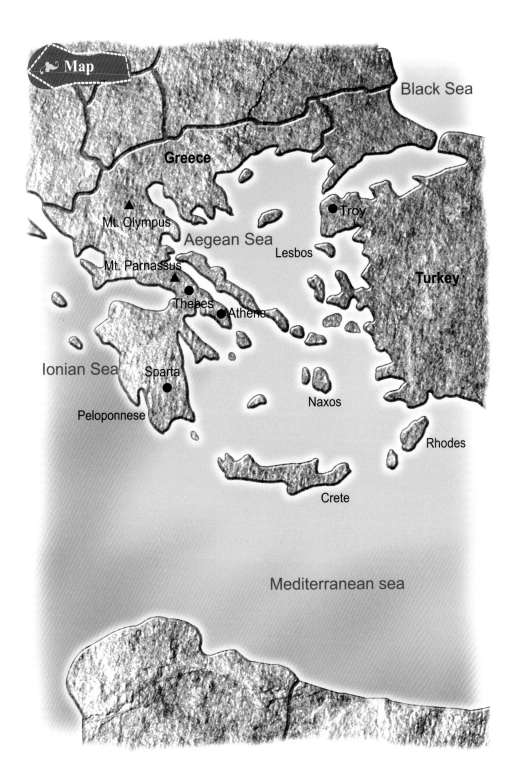

Map

Black Sea

Greece

Mt. Olympus

Aegean Sea

Mt. Parnassus

Troy

Lesbos

Turkey

Thebes

Athens

Ionian Sea

Sparta

Naxos

Peloponnese

Rhodes

Crete

Mediterranean sea

What will happen when a god and a human fall in love with each other?

What will happen when a human and an animal fall in love with each other?

This book contains mysterious stories of such kind.

One day, while Europa is at the seashore, Zeus sees her and falls in love with her at first sight. In order to approach the girl, he transforms into a bull, since he is a god, and Europa is a human. Out of curiosity, Europa climbs on the back of the bull, and then Zeus crosses the sea and reaches Crete Island. There, when Zeus reveals his true appearance, Europa begins to love him.

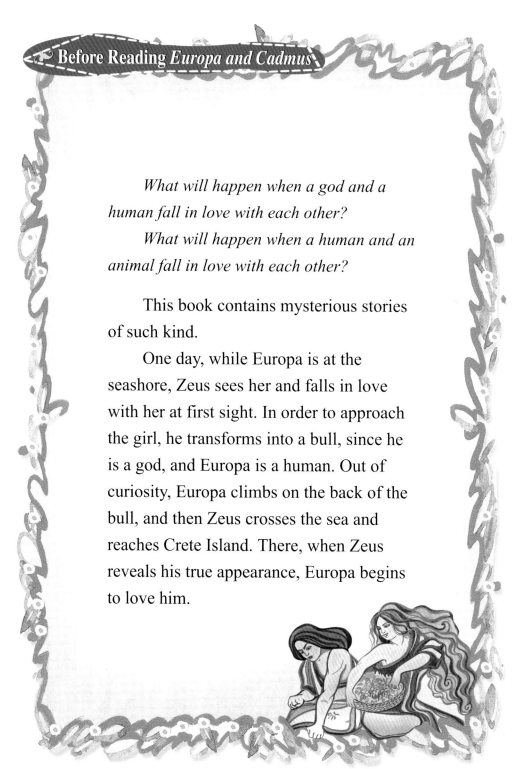

This book also contains another love story between a white bull and a human.

The story is about Pasiphae, wife of King Minos of Crete, who falls madly in love with a bull that Poseidon, the god of the sea, sent. How beautiful can a cow be to make a human fall in love with it?

Anyhow, Queen Pasiphae made love with the bull and gave birth to the Minotaur. However, the Minotaur was a fearsome monster, with a bull's head and a human's body. For a long time, he ended up living confined to the labyrinth that Daedalus built, until he was killed by the hero Theseus who came to the aid of Athenians.

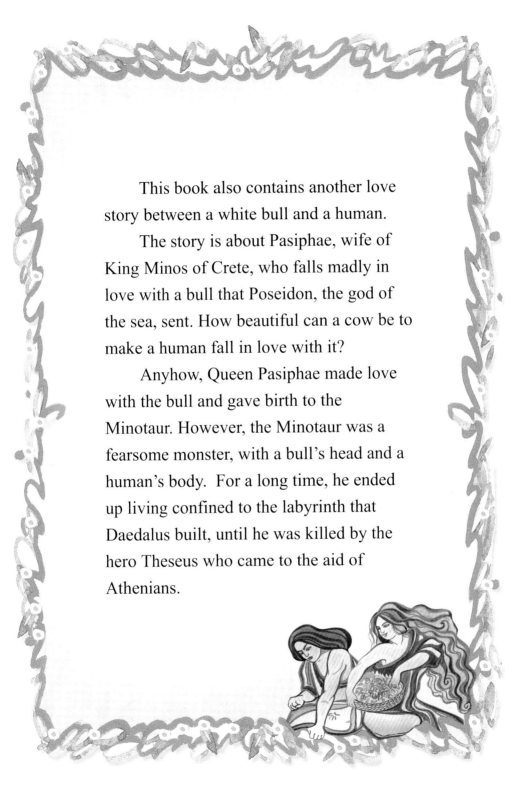

Europa

A Phoenician princess and the mother of King Minos. She is so beautiful that Zeus falls in love with her.

Cadmus

A Phoenician prince and the brother of Europa. He goes through many adventures, while setting out to look for his sister.

Harmonia

The wife of Cadmus and daughter of Aphrodite. Harmonia and Cadmus turn to snakes by Ares' curse.

Minos

The son of Europa and Cadmus, and the king of Crete. He is so arrogant that the god of the sea Poseidon lays a curse on him.

Pasiphae

The wife of King Minos, mother of Minotaur. She gives birth to a monster, the Minotaur, after falling in love with a white bull that Poseidon sent.

Minotaur

The Minotaur was born between Queen Pasiphae and a white bull. A monstrous half man half bull is so violent that it is confined to a labyrinth.

Daedalus

A famous craftsman who built a maze where the Minotaur was concealed.

Androgeus

The son of Minos and Pasiphae. After participating in the Athenian games, he gets murdered by Athenians.

Contents

Zeus and Europa ⸻10

Cadmus⸻19

Pasiphae and the Minotaur⸻39

Reading Comprehension⸻58

Europa was
a beautiful woman.
Her father was Agenor.
He was the king of
Phoenicia.
Everyday,
Europa left the castle.

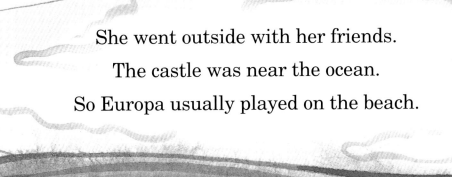

She went outside with her friends.

The castle was near the ocean.

So Europa usually played on the beach.

One day, Zeus saw Europa.

He fell in love with her.

Zeus wanted to meet her.

He had a good idea.

Zeus used his magic.

He became a white bull.

Europa and her friends were at the beach.

They were playing together.

Suddenly,

a white bull came out

of the ocean.

Europa looked at the bull.

She wanted to ride on it.

Europa on the White Bull

Europa climbed up onto the bull's back.

The bull walked around with Europa.

"This is fun. Now, I want to get off," she said.

Europa tried to get off the bull.

But the bull walked towards the ocean.

Suddenly, the bull ran into the water.

The bull was swimming in the water!

"Europa! Where are you going?
Come back!" shouted her friends.
Europa was scared.
She wanted to go back home.
But she couldn't get off the bull's back.

The bull swam for a long time.

Finally, the bull came to the island of Crete.

It was very far from Phoenicia.

"Why did you bring me here?"
Europa asked the bull.
But the bull was not there.
Now, there was a very handsome man, Zeus.

Soon, she fell in love with him.

Zeus and Europa lived on Crete for a long time.

Later, they had three sons together.

Their names were Minos, Rhadamanthys,

and Sarpedon.

Minos became the king of Crete.

Cadmus

Agenor was the king of Phoenicia.

He had a son and a daughter.

His son was Cadmus,

and his daughter was Europa.

One day, many women came into his castle.

"King! King! A white bull took Europa.

It swam across the ocean," they said.

Agenor was very upset and called his son Cadmus.

"You must go and find her.

Do not come back without her," he ordered.

Cadmus looked for Europa
for a long time.
He visited many countries.
He asked many people
about Europa.
But nobody saw Europa.
So he went to the city of Delphi.
A wise oracle lived there.

"Please, oracle, what should
I do?" asked Cadmus.
"You must leave this city,"
said the oracle.
"You will see a cow. Follow it.
Later, the cow will stop
walking," continued the oracle,
"You must build a city there.
You will call the city Thebes."
Cadmus thanked the oracle
and left Delphi.

23

One day, Cadmus saw a cow. Cadmus followed the cow for a long time. Finally, the cow stopped. "This is it! I will build my city here," said Cadmus, "I want to honor Zeus."

Cadmus called his servants and spoke to them.

"Go into that forest. Bring me back some water."

The servants found a pool in the forest.

The water was cold and pure.

But there was a cave next to the pool.

25

A giant serpent lived in the cave. It had long, sharp teeth. It breathed fire. Hissssssssssssssssss. The servants were very afraid. They couldn't move. The serpent killed all of the servants.

Cadmus waited and waited all day long for his men.
But they didn't come back.
So he went into the forest to find them.
He found the pool and his dead servants.
And he saw the serpent, too.
"My poor men. I will kill the serpent for you,"
he cried. Cadmus picked up a big rock and
threw it at the serpent.
But the serpent
was not hurt.

Then, Cadmus took out his spear.

He hit the serpent with the spear

many times.

But the serpent was strong.

Cadmus became very tired.

"Please, Zeus. Give me strength.

I must kill the serpent,"

Cadmus prayed.

Then Cadmus threw his spear

at the serpent.

The spear hit the serpent

in the head.

Then the serpent died.

Cadmus heard a strange voice.

"Take the serpent's teeth.

Sow them in the ground,"

said the voice.

He took the serpent's teeth.

Then, he sowed them all

in the ground.

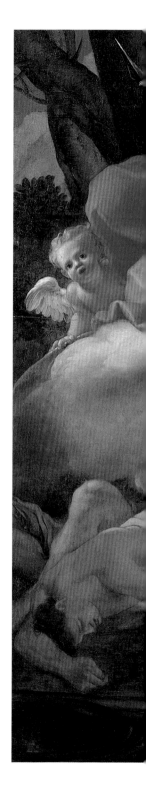

Cadmus Killing the Serpent

Suddenly, the ground was moving.

Spears came up from the earth.

Helmets came up from the earth.

Men were wearing the helmets!

Men were growing from the earth!

There were hundreds
of men now.

They all had
spears.

The men attacked each other.

All day long, the soldiers fought.

Soon, there were only five soldiers.

They stopped fighting and looked at Cadmus.

"You are our lord. We will help you," they said.

Cadmus and the five soldiers made a city.

They called it Thebes.

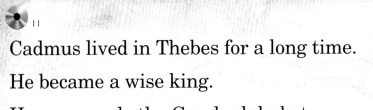

Cadmus lived in Thebes for a long time.

He became a wise king.

He even made the Greek alphabet.

Cadmus met a beautiful woman named Harmonia.

She is the goddess of harmony and concord.

Harmonia's mother was Aphrodite.

She is the goddess of beauty.

Cadmus and Harmonia got married.

All the gods were happy.

But only one god, Ares, was not happy.

He hated Cadmus.

The serpent had been Ares's pet.

34

Cadmus and Harmonia had two daughters.

They also had many grandchildren.

But one day, Ares used his magic.

He killed Cadmus's daughters.

Later, he killed Cadmus's grandchildren, too.

Cadmus and Harmonia were very sad.

They did not want to live in Thebes anymore.

So Cadmus and Harmonia left the city.

They traveled together for many months.

13 One day, they came to
a new country, Enchelia.
The people of Enchelia were very kind.
"Please, live in our country," they said.
Cadmus became the king of Enchelia.
But Cadmus was still very sad.
He remembered his children
and grandchildren.

'Why is a serpent so important? Why does Ares love a serpent?' Cadmus asked himself.

"The gods must love serpents.

Then I want to become a serpent," he said.

Suddenly, Cadmus became a serpent.

Harmonia saw this.

She loved Cadmus very much.

"I want to be a serpent, too!" she cried.

So Harmonia became a serpent, too.

Together, they lived in the forest forever.

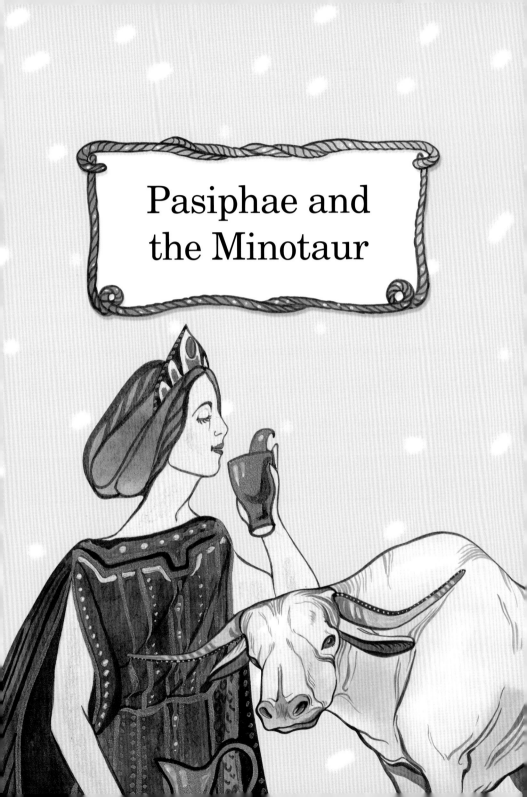

Pasiphae and the Minotaur

Minos was the son of Europa and Zeus.

He was also the king of Crete.

One day, Minos met a beautiful woman.

Her name was Pasiphae.

They got married.

And Pasiphae became a queen.

One night, there was a party.

Minos said, "I am a great man.

The gods always listen to me."

The people did not believe him.

"Why do the gods listen to you?" they asked.

"Watch! I will show you," said Minos.

The next day, Minos prepared
a sacrifice to Poseidon.
Minos prayed to Poseidon.
"Poseidon, send me a white bull.
I will sacrifice it to you," he said.

Suddenly, a white bull swam up from the water.

King Minos was very happy.

'This bull is too beautiful.

I cannot sacrifice it,' he thought.

So Minos sacrificed a different bull.

45

Poseidon became very angry.

Poseidon used his magic on Queen Pasiphae.

He made her fall in love with the white bull.

Now, she did not love Minos anymore.

Everyday, Pasiphae went to the barn.

Later, Pasiphae had a child.
It was not a person.
It was the Minotaur.
The Minotaur had a man's body
and a bull's head.
The Minotaur was always very
angry. And he ate people.

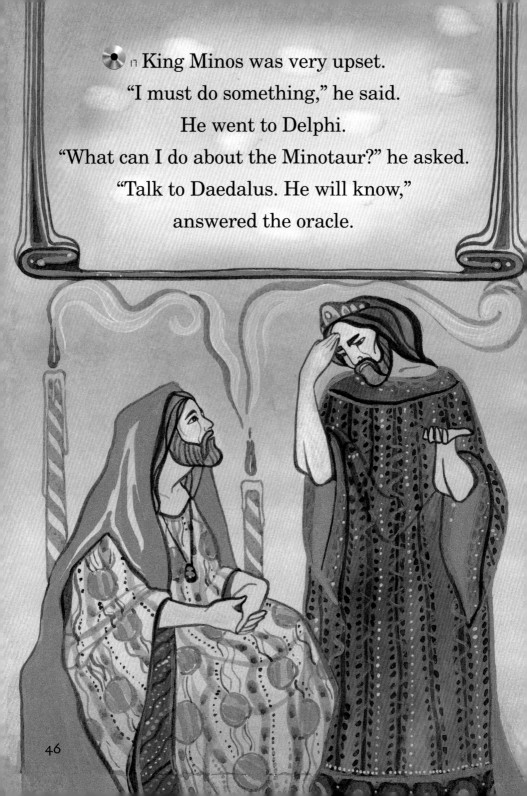

King Minos was very upset.

"I must do something," he said.

He went to Delphi.

"What can I do about the Minotaur?" he asked.

"Talk to Daedalus. He will know,"

answered the oracle.

Daedalus was the smartest man in the world.
He made many wonderful machines.
Actually, he could make anything.
Minos called Daedalus to his castle.
He asked Daedalus about the Minotaur.
"I'll build a maze," Daedalus said,
"Then you can put the Minotaur in it.
He will never come out."

47

Daedalus built the Labyrinth.

The Labyrinth was a giant maze.

Nobody could find the exit.

Minos put the Minotaur inside the Labyrinth.

But the Minotaur had to eat people.

So Minos put young men and women

in the Labyrinth, too.

The Minotaur in the Labyrinth

Minos and Pasiphae also had a son.

His name was Androgeus.

Once, he traveled to Athens.

There were many games in Athens.

Androgeus was very good at games.

He won all of the games.

The king of Athens, Aegeus, went to the games.
"Who is that man?
He is very good at sports," he said.
"His name is Androgeus from Crete.
His father is King Minos," someone answered.

🔘₂₀ King Aegeus became very angry.
"Only the people of Athens may play.
That man must die."
So many people attacked Androgeus
and killed him.

King Minos heard about this.

He was very sad and angry.

He wanted to punish Athens.

"People of Crete," he said,

"we must attack Athens."

Athens and Crete fought for a long time.

Then, Minos prayed to Zeus.

Zeus helped King Minos win the war.

The people of Athens were very afraid.

They went to Delphi.

"Zeus is helping Crete! What can we do?"
one person asked.

"Do anything for Minos," said the oracle.

The people of Athens asked Minos for peace.

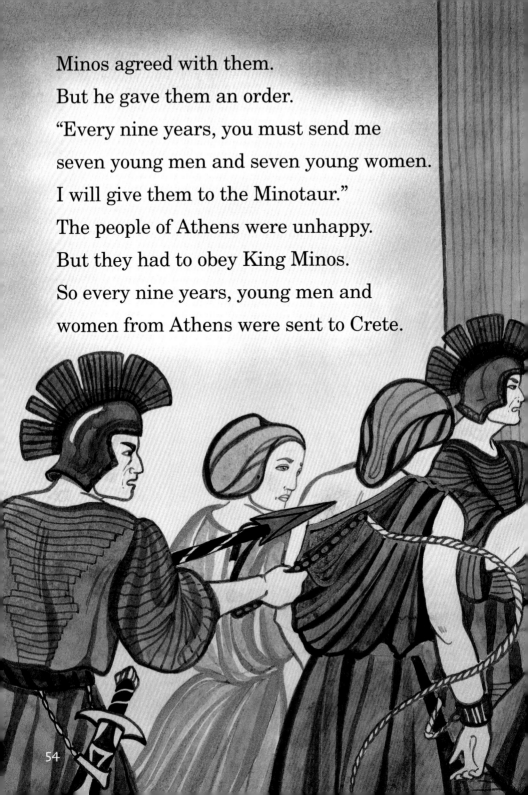

Minos agreed with them.

But he gave them an order.

"Every nine years, you must send me
seven young men and seven young women.

I will give them to the Minotaur."

The people of Athens were unhappy.

But they had to obey King Minos.

So every nine years, young men and
women from Athens were sent to Crete.

Europa and Europe

One night Europa had a dream.

She dreamed about two very big women.

These women were really continents.

One woman was Asia.

The other woman didn't have a name.

They were fighting because of Europa.

Asia said that Europa had been born in Asia,

so Europa belonged to Asia.

The other woman said

that Europa's birth place was not important.

So Zeus gave Europa to the second continent.

That is how its name became Europe.

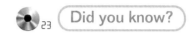

The Minotaur

King Minos kept the Minotaur in the Labyrinth.

The Labyrinth was a maze.

Every year,
14 Athenians
were sent
to Crete.
The Minotaur
would eat
them.

One year, brave Theseus came to Crete from Athens.

King Minos had a daughter, Ariadne.

She fell in love with Theseus.

She gave Theseus a ball of string.

Theseus went into the Labyrinth.

He tied one end of the string near the gate.

Then he found and killed the Minotaur.

He followed the string back to the gate.

Theseus saved Athenians from the Minotaur.

Reading Comprehension

Part 1

Zeus and Europa

Read the questions and choose the best answers.

1. Where is Europa's hometown?

   (A) Phoenicia   (B) Greece

   (C) Crete   (D) Egypt

2. Circle True or False.

   ■ Zeus became a black bull.

   True   False

   ■ The bull swam across the ocean.

   True   False

3. How many children did Europa have?

   (A) 1   (B) 2   (C) 3   (D) 4

Part 2

Cadmus

🎵 Read the questions, choose or write the best answers.

1. Who is Cadmus's sister?

2. What animal did Cadmus follow?

    (A) a bull   (B) a cow

    (C) a serpent   (D) a dog

3. Write the correct answer in the blank.

    The servants walked into a _____.

    They were looking for water.

    But a giant _____ killed all of them.

4. Why did Ares hate Cadmus?

    (A) Because Ares loved Harmonia.

    (B) Because the serpent had been his pet.

    (C) Because Ares wanted to make Thebes.

Part 3

Pasiphae and the Minotaur

 Read the questions and choose
the best answers.

1. Who is King Minos's wife?

2. Circle True or False.

■ Poseidon sent a white bull to King Minos.

   True   False

■ Pasiphae fell in love with Daedalus.

   True   False

3. Why did King Minos attack Athens?

   (A) Because the people of Athens killed his son.
   (B) Because he did not like King Aegeus.
   (C) Because he wanted more land.

4. What did Athens send to Crete every nine years?

   (A) the Minotaur
   (B) young men and women
   (C) white bulls

Europa and Cadmus

中譯解答本

卓加真　譯

神話用有趣的方式說明生命，各種故事解釋各種奇異或可怕現象，滿足人們的好奇心。世界上的每個民族，都有自己的神話。在神話的奇幻世界裡，人類可以化身成鳥或星辰。太陽、風、樹木等等，自然界萬物皆充滿了和人類互動頻繁的神靈。

希臘和羅馬神話的出現，已超過三千年，源自居住在地中海岸的希臘人。之後，再由義大利的羅馬人所接受，並進一步改寫之。

希臘神話的故事，大都與雲霄上的奧林帕斯山諸神有關。雲霧常為奧林帕斯山蒙上神祕的氣氛，古希臘人認為，神明就住在山上，其形體、感情和行為舉止，無異於人。希臘人和羅馬人建立寺廟、獻祭動物、祈禳，並用戲劇和運動競賽的方式，來取悅那些住在奧林帕斯山、與人同形同性的眾神。

世界最初是如何形成的？
為什麼會有晝夜之分？
為什麼會有四季變化？
人死後將從何而去？

閱讀希臘羅馬神話，可以幫助我們瞭解早期人類的世界觀。又因許多西方思想乃源自於希臘人和羅馬人，故窺視希臘羅馬神話，將有助於塑造出那些古文化的真貌。瞭解這些神話的內容，將可以讓人們對這個世界別有一番趣解。

神要是和凡人相戀，會有什麼下場？
凡人如果和動物相愛，又會有什麼後果？

這本書，將告訴你這種不可思議的故事！

有一天，宙斯一看到海邊的歐羅巴，就愛上了她。天神宙斯為了接近凡人歐羅巴，便化身成一頭公牛。歐羅巴看到公牛，覺得很好玩，就爬上了公牛的背上。結果，她被宙斯背著橫越海洋，來到了克里特島。宙斯在那裡變回原貌，歐羅巴看到他，也愛上了他。

本書還講了另外一個白牛與凡人相戀的故事。

克里特島國王麥諾斯的妻子巴喜菲，愛上了海神波賽墩所賜的一頭白公牛。一頭牛要長得多壯美，才能讓一個人類愛上牠呢？總之，巴喜菲皇后是愛上了牠，還為牠生下了牛頭人。但牛頭人是一頭可怕的怪物，長得牛頭人身的。有好長一段時間，牛頭人被關進戴達勒斯所建造的迷宮裡。後來，英雄鐵修斯前來幫助雅典人，他殺死了住在迷宮中的牛頭人，結束了他的生命。

目錄

● 中文翻譯與單字注釋…… 4

● 閱讀測驗…… 25

宙斯與歐羅巴

p. 10

歐羅巴是位美麗的女子，
其父為艾吉諾，
他是菲尼沙的國王。
歐羅巴每天都會出去皇宮外面。

- **everyday** [ˈev.ri.deɪ]
  每一天
- **left** [left] 離開
  （leave的過去式）
- **castle** [ˈkæs.l] 城堡

---

p. 11

她會和友人一起出宮。
因為皇宮就位於海邊，
所以她常在海灘上遊玩。

- **outside** [ˌaʊtˈsaɪd] 外面
- **ocean** [ˈoʊ.ʃən]
  大海；海洋
- **usually** [ˈju:.ʒu.ə.li]
  通常；按照慣例地
- **beach** [bi:tʃ] 海灘

---

p. 12

有一日，宙斯看見歐羅巴，
一見鍾情愛上她。
宙斯想認識她，就想了一個辦法。
他運用法術，
變成一隻乳白色的公牛。

- **fall in love with**
  [fɑ:l ɪn lʌv wɪð]
  愛上；對……產生感情
- **use** [ju:z] 使用；利用
- **magic** [ˈmædʒ.ɪk]
  魔法；法術
- **bull** [bʊl] 公牛

p. 13

歐羅巴和友伴在海邊一起玩樂，
突然，一隻白色的公牛從海上出現。
歐羅巴看著公牛，
想騎上牛背。

- **together** [təˋgeð.ə]
  一起；共同
- **suddenly** [ˋsʌd.ˀn.li]
  突然地
- **ride** [raɪd]
  騎；乘

p. 14

歐羅巴爬到公牛背上，
公牛載著歐羅巴四處漫步。
「真好玩。現在，我想下來了。」
她說。
她準備爬下牛背，
但公牛卻走向海洋。
突然間，公牛飛也似地衝進水中，
在水裡游泳前進！

- **climb** [klaɪm] 爬；攀登
- **back** [bæk] 背
- **try to** [traɪ tə] 嘗試
- **get off** [get a:f]
  （從牛馬、車上）下來；
  離開
- **towards** [tuˋwɔːrdz]
  向；朝

p. 15

「歐羅巴！妳要去哪裡？
快回來呀！」友人叫著她。
歐羅巴很害怕，
她想回家，
但沒辦法爬下公牛背。

- **come back** [kʌm bæk]
  回來
- **shout** [ʃaʊt] 大叫；叫喊
- **scared** [skerd]
  驚恐的；恐懼的

- -

 p. 16

公牛游行了許久，
最後來到克里特島。
這裡離菲尼沙很遠。

- **finally** [ˋfaɪ.nə.li]
  最終；最後
- **island** [ˋaɪ.lənd] 島
- **far** [fɑːr] 遠

- -

 p. 17

「你為什麼要帶我來這裡？」
歐羅巴問公牛。
但公牛卻消失不見，
眼前只見俊美的宙斯。

- **bring** [brɪŋ] 帶
- **ask** [æsk] 問；詢問
- **handsome** [ˋhæn.səm]
  好看的；英俊的

p. 18

歐羅巴很快愛上他。

他們兩人在島上生活了許久，

生下了三個兒子，

分別是麥諾斯、拉達曼策斯和撒柏頓。

麥諾斯後來成為克里特島的國王。

- **later** [leɪtə] 後來
- **their** [ðer] 他（她）們的（they的所有格）
- **son** [sʌn] 兒子
- **became** [bɪˋkeɪm] 變成（become的過去式）

卡德莫斯

p. 20

艾吉諾是菲尼沙的國王，

膝下有一子一女。

兒子名為卡德莫斯，

女兒即歐羅巴。

- **daughter** [ˋdɑ:ˏtə] 女兒

p. 21

這天，幾個女子走進皇宮，說道：

「國王陛下！

歐羅巴讓一隻白色公牛給帶走，

往海裡走去了。」

艾吉諾很慌張，叫來兒子卡德莫斯，

命令道：「你去把她找回來，

找不到她，你也別回來了！」

- **swam** [swæm] 游泳（swim的過去式）
- **across** [əˋkrɑ:s] 橫越；到對面
- **upset** [ʌpˋset] 心煩意亂的；沮喪的
- **order** [ˋɔ:r.də] 命令

卡德莫斯四處尋找歐羅巴。

他遊歷許多國家，也問了許多人，

就是沒有歐羅巴的消息。

因此他來到狄菲城，

那裡住了一位能解神諭的智者。

- **look for** [lʊk fə] 尋找
- **nobody** [ˋnoʊ.bɑː.di]
  誰也不；沒人
- **country** [ˋkʌn.tri]
  郡；縣；國家
- **saw** [sɑː] 看見
  （see的過去式）
- **Delphi** [ˋdɛlfaɪ] 狄菲神
  殿（希臘古都；有以宣
  示神諭著名稱的Apollo
  神殿）
- **wise** [waɪz]
  聰明的；有智慧的
- **oracle** [ˋɔ:r.ə.kl]
  聖人；先知

「神媒，請告訴我該怎麼辦？」

卡德莫斯問著。

神媒回答：「離開這個城市，

你會看到一頭母牛，跟著牠走。

之後，這頭牛會停下來，

你要在那裡建立一座城市，

將城市命名為底比斯。」

卡德莫斯辭謝了神媒，離開狄菲城。

- **should** [ʃʊd] 應該
- **leave** [li:v] 離開
- **cow** [kaʊ] 母牛；乳牛
- **follow** [ˋfɑː.loʊ] 跟隨
- **continue** [kənˋtɪn.ju:]
  繼續
- **build** [bɪld] 建造；建築
- **thank** [θæŋk] 道謝

p. 24

有一天，卡德莫斯看到一頭母牛，
便跟著這頭牛走了許久，
終於，牛停下來了。
卡德莫斯說：「就是這裡！
我將在這裡建立屬於我城市，
我要榮耀宙斯。」

- **honor** [ˋɑː.nɚ]
  向……致意

---

p. 25

卡德莫斯喚來手下，對他們說：
「到森林裡去，找些水回來。」
隨從們在森林中發現一個池子，
池水冰冷而純淨，
池邊還有一個洞穴。

- **servant** [ˋsɜː.vᵊnt]
  僕人；傭人
- **forest** [ˋfɔːr.ɪst] 森林
- **found** [faʊnd]
  找到；發現
  （find的過去式）
- **pool** [puːl] 池塘
- **pure** [pjʊr] 純淨的
- **cave** [keɪv] 山洞；洞穴
- **next to** [nekst tə]
  在……隔壁

洞裡住著一條巨蟒，
牠的毒牙又長又尖銳，
嘴裡不時噴著火焰，
還發出嘶嘶的聲音。
眾人驚慌失措，
怕得手軟腳軟動不了。
巨蟒於是就這樣殺了所有的隨從。

- **giant** [ˋdʒaɪ.ᵊnt] 巨大的
- **serpent** [ˋsɜ:.pᵊnt]
  巨蛇；惡魔
- **sharp** [ʃɑ:rp] 尖銳的
- **breathe** [bri:ð] 呼吸
- **hiss** [hɪs] 嘶嘶聲

卡德莫斯枯等一整天，
仍不見手下回來，
於是便走進森林找他們。
他來到池子邊，
看到已經氣絕的手下，
也看到了巨蟒。
「我死去的弟兄啊，我要爲你們報仇！」
他喊道。
卡德莫斯舉起一塊巨石，
朝巨蟒丟去。
但巨蟒卻毫髮無傷。

- **wait** [weɪt] 等待
- **all day long**
  [ɑ:l deɪ lɑ:ŋ] 一整天
- **dead** [ded] 死亡的
- **poor** [pʊr] 池塘
- **cry** [kraɪ] 大叫；呼喊
- **pick up** [pɪk ʌp]
  拾起；撿起
- **threw** [θru:]
  扔向；擲向
  （throw的過去式）
- **hurt** [hɜ:t] 受傷

p. 28

接著，卡德莫斯執起長矛，
猛刺巨蟒。
巨蟒力大無窮，
卡德莫斯幾乎精力耗盡。
「宙斯，請賜給我力量，
我一定要殺了這條巨蟒！」
卡德莫斯禱告著。
接著卡德莫斯擲出長矛，
正中了巨蟒的頭部，
巨蟒應聲而倒。
卡德莫斯這時聽到一陣奇怪的聲音，
說道：「拔取巨蟒之牙，
將牙種在土裡。」
於是他拔下巨蟒的牙齒，
把牙齒種在土裡。

- **spear** [spɪr] 矛
- **hit** [hɪt] 擊中
- **strong** [strɑːŋ]
  強壯的
- **tired** [taɪr] 精疲力盡的
- **strength** [streŋθ] 力量
- **pray** [preɪ] 祈禱
- **strange** [streɪndʒ]
  奇怪的；不可思議的
- **voice** [vɔɪs] 聲音
- **sow** [soʊ] 播種
- **ground** [graʊnd]
  地上的；地面的

11

p. 30

這時，大地突然震動起來。

土地上長出長矛，

長出戰盔，

也長出了人！

他們披甲戴盔，

人數達數百人，

各持執長矛。

- **move** [muːv] 搖動；震動
- **helmet** [hel.mət] 頭盔
- **grow** [groʊ] 長出
- **hundreds of**
  [ˋhʌn.drəds ɑːv]
  數以千計的

---

p. 31

這些人互相攻擊，

打了一整日，

最後，只剩下五名戰士。

他們停下來，看著卡德莫斯，

齊口同聲道：

「我們尊你為王，全力協助你！」

卡德莫斯便與五名戰士，

共同建立了一個新城市，

名為底比斯。

- **attack** [əˋtæk] 攻擊
- **each other** [iːtʃ ˋʌð.ə]
  互相；彼此
- **soldier** [ˋsoʊl.dʒə] 士兵
- **fought** [fɑːt] 作戰；打鬥
  (fight的過去式)
- **lord** [lɔːrd] 首領；大王

p. 32

卡德莫斯在底比斯住了很長一段時間，
他是一個賢明的君主，
還創造了希臘字母。
他遇見一位名叫哈夢妮亞的美麗女子，
她是和諧女神，
她的母親是美麗女神阿芙柔黛蒂。

- **Greek** [gri:k] 希臘的
- **alphabet** [ˈæl.fə.bet] 字母表
- **named** [neɪmd] 名為
- **goddess** [ˈgɑː.des] 女神
- **harmony** [ˈhɑːr.mə.ni] 和諧
- **concord** [ˈkɑːn.kɔːrd] 一致
- **beauty** [ˈbjuːt̬i] 美

---

p. 33

卡德莫斯和哈夢妮亞共結連理，
眾神歡欣慶祝，
只有戰神阿瑞士心中不悅。
他憎恨卡德莫斯，
因為那條巨蟒就是阿瑞士的寵物。

- **got married** [gɑːt ˈmer.id] 結婚
- **hate** [heɪt] 憎恨；厭惡
- **pet** [pet] 寵物

卡德莫斯和哈夢妮亞育有二女，
也有許多孫子。
然而有一天，阿瑞士以他的神力，
殺了卡德莫斯的兩位女兒和孫子。

* **grandchildren**
  [ˋgrænd.tʃɪl.drən]
  曾孫們

卡德莫斯與哈夢妮亞哀慟不已，
他們不想再留在底比斯，
便離開了這個城市，
一起在外飄蕩了數個月。

* **anymore** [ˌen.iˋmɔːr]
  而今再也（用於否定句
  或疑問句中）
* **travel** [ˋvræv.əl]
  旅行；漂流
* **month** [mʌntθ] 月份

這一天，他們來到一個新生的國家，
名為安切利亞。
當地人民非常友善，
「請在我們這裡住下吧！」他們說。
卡德莫斯於是成為安切利亞的國王，

* **kind** [kaɪnd]
  親切的；友善的
* **still** [stɪl] 仍然
* **sad** [sæd] 悲傷
* **remember** [rɪˋmem.bə]
  記起；回憶起

但他內心仍然哀傷，
時時想起自己的孩子和孫子。

---

p. 38

「何以巨蟒如此重要？
何以阿瑞士如此鍾愛巨蟒？」
卡德莫斯自問自答道：
「眾神必定喜愛巨蟒，
那麼，就讓我能成為一條蟒蛇吧！」
話才說完，他突然就變成了蟒蛇！
哈夢妮亞目睹了這一切，
她深愛著卡德莫斯，便喊道：
「我願隨他變成蟒蛇！」
於是哈夢妮亞也變成了蟒蛇，
他們一起住在森林，直到永遠。

- **important** [ɪm`pɔːr.t̬ənt]
  重要的
- **ask oneself**
  [æsk wʌn`self] 問自己
- **suddenly** [`sʌd.ən.li]
  突然地
- **forever** [fɔ:`rev.ə]
  永遠地

巴喜菲與牛頭人怪物

 p. 40

麥諾斯是歐羅巴與宙斯之子，
他是克里特島的國王。
有一天，
麥諾斯遇見一位叫巴喜菲的美麗女子。
他們後來結了婚，
所以巴喜菲就成為了皇后。

- **also** [`ɑːl.soʊ] 亦；也
- **queen** [kwiːn]
  皇后；女王

---

 p. 41

一天夜裡，在一場舞會中，
麥諾斯說：「我是個偉人，
眾神都要聽命於我。」
在場人士不相信他的話。
「何以眾神需聽命於你？」他們問道。
「仔細瞧，我將證明給你們看！」
麥諾斯說。

- **great** [greɪt] 偉大的
- **listen to** [`lɪs.ᵊn tə]
  聽從；傾聽
- **believe** [brˋliːv] 相信
- **watch** [wɑːtʃ]
  看著；注視
- **show** [ʃoʊ]
  證實；表現出

隔天，
麥諾斯準備祭品要獻給海神波賽墩，
他向海神祈禱道：
「海神啊，請賜給我一頭白公牛，
我會將公牛獻祭給你！」

- **prepare** [prɪˋper] 準備
- **sacrifice** [ˋsæk.ri.faɪs] 獻祭；供奉

突然間，一頭白色公牛從水中游出，
麥諾斯國王很歡喜，心忖道：
「這頭公牛真美，
我不能把牠獻祭給你。」
麥諾斯便獻上了另一頭牛。

- **sacrifice** [ˋsæk.ri.faɪs] 準備
- **thought** [θɑːt] 思考著（think的過去式）
- **different** [ˋdɪf.ɚ.ᵊnt] 不同的；不一樣的

波賽墩因此大為震怒，
對他的皇后巴喜菲施了魔法，
讓她愛上這頭白色公牛。
於是她變得不再愛麥諾斯，
每天都跑去穀倉找白公牛。

- **angry** [ˋæŋ.gri] 生氣；憤怒
- **magic** [ˋmædʒ.ɪk] 魔法；法術
- **made** [meɪd] 使成為……（make的過去式）
- **everyday** [ˋev.ri.deɪ] 每一天

* **went** [went] 去
  （go的過去式）
* **barn** [bɑ:rn] 穀倉

---

 p. 45

後來，皇后巴喜菲生下了一個孩子，

這個孩子長得不像人類，

而是長得牛頭人身的。

他的身體像人，頭長得像牛，

他很容易發怒，而且還會吃人。

* **person** [ˋpɝ.sən] 人類
* **ate** [et] 吃
  （eat的過去式）

---

 p. 46

麥諾斯國王很生氣，他說道：

「我一定要想個辦法！」

他來到狄菲城，問道：

「我該怎麼對付這個牛頭人？」

神媒答道：

「去問戴達勒斯吧，他有辦法！」

* **upset** [ʌpˋset]
  心煩意亂的
* **something** [ˋsʌm.θɪŋ]
  某些事情
* **must** [mʌst] 必須；一定
* **answer** [ˋænt.sɚ] 回答

戴達勒斯是世上最有智慧的人。
他創造了許多驚奇的機械，
他是個全能的工匠，什麼都會做。
麥諾斯將戴達勒斯召喚入宮。
向他請教該如何對付牛頭人。
戴達勒斯說：「我會建造一座迷宮，
你可以把牛頭人關入迷宮，
他就永遠出不來了。」

- **smartest** [smɑ:rt]
  最有智慧的；最聰明的
  （smart聰明的，smarter
  較聰明的）
- **wonderful** [ˈwʌn.də.fəl]
  不可思議的；
  令人驚奇的
- **machine** [məˈʃi:n] 機器
- **actually** [ˈæk.tʃu.əli]
  事實上
- **maze** [meɪz] 迷宮

戴達勒斯於是建造了賴比瑞斯迷宮。
這是一座巨型迷宮，
沒有人可以找到出口。
麥諾斯把牛頭人關入迷宮，
但這怪物以人為食，
因此麥諾斯將年輕男女一道關入迷宮。

- **labyrinth** [ˈlæb.ə.rɪnθ]
  迷宮；曲徑
- **nobody** [ˈnou.bɑ:.di]
  誰也不；無人
- **exit** [ˈek.sɪt] [ˈeg.zɪt]
  出口
- **inside** [ɪnˈsaɪd]
  在…的內部
- **eat** [i:t] 吃
- **people** [ˈpi:.pl] 人類
- **young** [jʌn]
  年輕的；幼小的

p. 49

麥諾斯和巴喜菲育有一子，
名為安德羅鳩士。
安德羅鳩士曾經遊歷雅典城，
雅典城中多有競技賽，
他是個中翹楚，
戰無不勝。

- **game** [geɪm]
  競技會；賽會
- **Athens** [ˋæθɪnz]
  雅典（希臘首都）
- **be good at** [bi ɡʊd ət]
  擅長於……；
  對……拿手
- **won** [wʌn] 勝利；贏
  （win的過去式）

p. 50

雅典國王愛琴士親臨競賽會場。
「這年輕人是誰？
他對運動非常擅長。」他說。
「他是克里特島來的安德羅鳩士，
他父親就是麥諾斯國王。」
有人回答道。

- **sport** [spɔːrt] 運動；
  體育競技活動
- **someone** [ˋsʌm.wʌn]
  某人

p. 51

愛琴士國王頓時大怒。

「只有雅典城的人才能參賽，

把這個年輕人處死！」

許多人便襲擊安德羅鳩士，

將他置之死地。

- **only** [ˋoun.li]
  唯一的；僅有的
- **may** [meɪ]
  可以（表示許可）
- **play** [pleɪ] 進行（比賽）
- **attack** [əˋtæk] 攻擊

p. 52

國王麥諾斯聽到兒子的死訊，

又悲痛又憤怒。

他要懲罰雅典人。

「克里特島的人民，

「我們要進攻雅典城！」他說。

於是兩方大戰許久，

最後麥諾斯向宙斯祈禱，

在宙斯的幫助下，

麥諾斯國王打贏了這一戰。

- **heard** [hɝd] 聽說；聽聞
  （hear的過去式）
- **punish** [ˋpʌn.ɪʃ] 懲罰
- **war** [wɔːr] 戰爭；戰役

p. 53

雅典城民非常害怕，
他們來到狄菲城。
「克里特島有宙斯在保佑！
我們該怎麼辦？」
其中一人問道。
「向麥諾斯屈服吧！」神諭指示道。
雅典人於是向麥諾斯國王求和。

- **anything** [ˈen.i.θɪŋ] 任何事物
- **ask** [æsk] 尋求
- **peace** [piːs] 和平

p. 54

麥諾斯接受求和，
但他下令道：「每隔九年，
你們必須送上七名童男、七名童女，
獻給牛頭人！」
雅典城民聽得人心忡忡，
但又不得不遵守命令。
因此，每隔九年，
雅典城民都會將童男童女，
送來克里特島。

- **agree** [əˈɡriː] 應允
- **every** [ˈev.ri] 每一；每個
- **unhappy** [ʌnˈhæp.i] 不開心的
- **obey** [oʌˈbeɪ] 服從；聽話
- **were sent** [wɚ sent] 被派遣

p. 56 (Did you know?)

歐羅巴（Europa）和歐洲（Europe）

有天晚上，歐羅巴做了個夢，
她夢到兩個體型巨碩的女人，
這兩名女子是兩片大陸塊。
其中一位名字叫做亞洲（Asia），
另一位則沒有名字。
她們兩個正在為歐羅巴一事而爭吵，
亞洲說，歐羅巴是在亞洲所生的，
因此屬於亞洲。
另一名女子說，
歐羅巴在哪裡出生並不重要。
最後，
宙斯把歐羅巴給了第二塊陸地，
而這也就是歐洲 Europe
這個詞的由來了。

- **dream** [dri:m] 夢
- **continent** [ˋkɑ:n.ṭn.ənt] 大陸地
- **Asia** [ˋeɪ.ʒə] 亞洲
- **be born in** [bi bɔ:rn ɪn] 出生……
- **belong** [bɪˋlɑ:ŋ] 屬於
- **birth place** [bɜ:θ pleɪs] 出生地
- **second** [ˋsek.ənd] 第二（個）的

牛頭人

麥諾斯國王把牛頭人關在迷宮裡，
賴比瑞斯是一座迷宮，
每年，雅典城民會送來十四名人質，
供怪物食用。

有一年，
英勇的鐵修斯從雅典來到克里特島。
麥諾斯國王有個女兒，
名叫亞莉阿德妮。
她愛上鐵修斯，
所以給了他一團線球。
鐵修斯進入迷宮，
將線的一端綁在入口附近，
接著他找到牛頭人，殺了他，
然後他再沿著線走出迷宮。
鐵修斯拯救雅典城民免於怪物之口。

- **kept** [kept] 使繼續保持
  （keep的過去式）
- **escape** [ɪˋskeɪp] 逃脫
- **Athenian** [əˋθnɪən]
  雅典人
- **brave** [breɪv] 勇敢的
- **ball of string**
  [bɑːl ɑːv strɪŋ] 一團線
- **string** [strɪŋ]
  細線；繩子
- **tie** [taɪ] 綁；緊緊

閱讀測驗

Part 1 .... p. 58

宙斯與歐羅巴

※ 閱讀下列問題並選出最適當的答案。

1. 歐羅巴的故鄉是哪裡？

(A) 菲尼沙　　　　(B) 希臘
(C) 克里特島　　　(D) 埃及

答案 (A)

2. 請圈選出正確或錯誤。

■ 宙斯變身成為一頭黑公牛。

True　　　　（False）

答案 False

■ 這頭公牛游泳橫跨過大海。

（True）　　　　False

答案 True

3. 歐羅巴總共有多少子嗣？

(A) 1　　　　(B) 2
(C) 3　　　　(D) 4

答案 (C)

※ 閱讀下列問題，並用選出或寫下正確的英文答案。

1. 卡德莫斯的妹妹是誰？

Europa

答案 歐羅巴

2. 卡德莫斯跟著哪一種動物走？

(A) 一頭公牛　　　(B) 一頭母牛

(C) 一條巨蟒　　　(D) 一隻狗

答案 (B)

3. 請在空白處填上正確的句子。

隨從們走進 <u>forest</u> 裡。

答案 森林

他們正在找水。

但是一條巨大的 <u>serpent</u> 把他們全殺光了。

答案 蟒蛇

4. 爲什麼阿瑞士痛恨卡德莫斯？

(A) 因爲阿瑞士喜愛哈夢妮亞

(B) 因爲這條巨莽是阿瑞士的寵物。　　　答案 (B)

(C) 因爲阿瑞士想要創建底比斯城。

Part 3

p. 60

巴喜菲與牛頭人

※ 閱讀下列問題，並選出最適當的答案。

1. 麥諾斯王的妻子是誰？

Pasiphae　　　　　　　　　　　答案 巴喜菲

2. 請圈選正確或錯誤。

■ 波賽墩將白牛送給麥諾斯國王。

(True)　　　　　False　　　　答案 True

■ 巴喜菲愛上了戴達勒斯。

True　　　　　(False)　　　　答案 False

27

3. 爲什麼麥諾斯國王要攻擊雅典呢？

(A) 因爲雅典城的人民殺了他的兒子。

答案 (A)

(B) 因爲他討厭愛琴士國王。

(C) 因爲他想要更多土地。

4. 每九年雅典城都會送上什麼到克里特島？

(A) 牛頭人怪物。

答案 (B)

(B) 童男童女。

(C) 白色公牛。

故事原著作者 Thomas Bulfinch

Without a knowledge of mythology much of the elegant literature of our own language cannot be understood and appreciated.

缺少了神話知識，就無法了解和透徹語言的文學之美。

—*Thomas Bulfinch*

Thomas Bulfinch（1796-1867），出生於美國麻薩諸塞州的Newton，隨後全家移居波士頓，父親為知名的建築師Charles Bulfinch。他在求學時期，曾就讀過一些優異的名校，並於1814年畢業於哈佛。

畢業後，執過教鞭，爾後從商，但經濟狀況一直未能穩定。1837年，在銀行擔任一般職員，以此為終身職業。後來開始進一步鑽研古典文學，成為業餘作家，一生未婚。

1855年，時值59歲，出版了奠立其作家地位的名作 *The Age of Fables*，書中蒐集希臘羅馬神話，廣受歡迎。此書後來與日後出版的 *The Age of Chivalry*（1858）和 *Legends of Charlemagne*（1863），合集更名為 *Bulfinch's Mythology*。

本系列書系，即改編自 *The Age of Fable*。Bulfinch 著寫本書時，特地以成年大眾為對象，以將古典文學引介給一般大眾。*The Age of Fable* 堪稱十九世紀的羅馬神話故事的重要代表著作，其中有很多故事來源，來自Bulfinch自己對奧維德（Ovid）的《變形記》（*Metamorphoses*）的翻譯。

■Bulfinch的著作

1. Hebrew Lyrical History.
2. The Age of Fable: Or Stories of Gods and Heroes.
3. The Age of Chivalry.
4. The Boy Inventor: A Memoir of Matthew Edwards, Mathematical-Instrument Maker.
5. Legends of Charlemagne.
6. Poetry of the Age of Fable.
7. Shakespeare Adapted for Reading Classes.
8. Oregon and Eldorado.
9. Bulfinch's Mythology: Age of Fable, Age of Chivalry, Legends of Charlemagne.